MW00777949

All Messy

A book of short stories

DENISE D. GIBSON

This publication contains the opinions and ideas of its author. It is intended to provide helpful and informative material on the subjects addressed in the publication. The author and publisher specifically disclaim all responsibility for any liability, loss, or risk, personal or otherwise, which is incurred as a consequence, directly or indirectly, of the use and application of any of the contents of this book.

WRITERS REPUBLIC L.L.C.
515 Summit Ave. Unit R1
Union City, NJ 07087, USA

Website: *www.writersrepublic.com*
Hotline: *1-877-656-6838*
Email: *info@writersrepublic.com*

Ordering Information:
Quantity sales. Special discounts are available on quantity purchases by corporations, associations, and others. For details, contact the publisher at the address above.

Library of Congress Control Number: 2020912348
ISBN-13:   978-1-64620-435-9   [Paperback Edition]
                  978-1-64620-436-6   [Digital Edition]

Rev. date: 07/01/2020

Contents

For my mom, she spills the funniest tea.

Introduction

Short stories are tiny windows into other worlds and other minds and other dreams. They are journeys you can make to the far side of the universe and still be back in time for dinner.
—Neil Gaiman

The great thing about a short story is that it doesn't have to trawl through someone's whole life; it can come in glancingly from the side.
—Emma Donoghue

Crawling out of a dilemma and its challenges can be a drag, according to a sketchy character, teenage Mona in "Confession." It can end a friendship forever. If you ask Val in "Death to Ms. Valentine," she thought she had the perfect ride out of her marriage until her car gave out. A mother, Babs, in "A Request from a Stranger," gets confronted with her past and the heartache it has caused. There are other episodes in this book where the characters find themselves dealing with sticky occurrences. They all tend to be so deeply involved in their problems that they struggle with finding a logical solution.

Watching the characters experience these situations is cringeworthy and can warrant empathy, but beware of their schemes. The stories are filled with the gossipy amusement that keeps people following media, reality television, and hearsay.

If you have gone to school and had a clique of friends, fell in love, or made an embarrassing mistake, you may understand how some of these characters feel. Maybe you know a better way to resolve their awkward situations.

Confession

Mona, a petite teen, sits cross-legged on a twin-size bed in a dark almost-bare room. Her chocolate-bronzed fingers comb through the spiraled ebony ringlets of her hair in an up-swoop motion to tie it with a black elastic band in a loose ponytail. The moon spotlights through a foggy nine-by-twelve-inches window onto a notebook in her lap while she writes and glares at one blank page. Her right hand translates her thoughts into scribbles onto the blue lines. She pauses and squints at the page while chewing on the cap of the ink pen.

October 15, 2010

Dear Diary,

I have a confession: I have had a crush on Nathan Brooks since the beginning of freshmen year, but I guess the timing is not right yet for us to be together. But there is more to this story…

It started when my best friend, Crystal, and I were at our high school football pep rally, cheering and feeling the school spirit. From our bleacher seats, we watched our principal announce the players one by one as they ran out to make their appearance for the crowd.

"He's our MVP…our underdog running back…give it up for Adam Scott!" Mr. Howard announced on the microphone.

The crowd cheered and clapped as Adam did a light jog from the locker room to the center of the gym and waved at the crowd.

Crystal and I glanced over Adam's slim yet chiseled physique that showed through his navy Hillman High football T-shirt and light-blue fitted jeans.

"Adam is cute. I think I'm going to love high school," Crystal shouted into her hands, cupped over my ear to make her audible over the noise.

I smiled and nodded yes in response.

"And now, he took us in to the championship last year…he's your favorite quarterback! He's Nathan-n-n-n Bro-o-o-k-k-k-s-s-s!" the principal enthusiastically proclaimed.

The crowd went wild. The sounds of cheering, whistling, stomping of feet, and clapping filled the gym.

A six-foot medium-brown-skinned guy suavely trotted to the center of the gym.

Crystal and I paused our clapping when we noticed him. We were both in awe at the sight of his manly carved jawline, his wide smile that gleamed bright, his dark-brown eyes, and his fresh Caesar haircut. He looked at the crowd and gave a humble grin and wave. Then his stance turned to his teammates and gave hugs with handshakes. The other football players' eyes held an awe-stricken gaze as Nathan acknowledged them player by player.

Nathan's left earring gleamed brightly, which drew more attention to the sight of him as he conducted small pep talks with the other players.

That was when my crush on Nathan started.

Wow! I cannot believe I remember all that from my freshman year.

Freshman and sophomore years in school were great. Crystal and I became sort of popular. We never missed a gathering, and the excitement and fun always started when we showed up. Not until the summer after freshman year, we realized the impact we had on people. Some girls got curly perm treatments to match my natural coils. Other girls started going to the same nail salon as Crystal to match her nail designs. Of course, our new sense of notoriety led us to being close with Nate. Oh yeah, I started calling him that one day, and he loved it! So the name stuck, and it's all because of me.

I dated a little. I hid many of my relationships from Nate though. It would've been awful to break his heart to see I wasn't holding out for him.

On a random school day…

"Why won't you hold my hand in the hallway, baby?" Adam sweetly whispered in my ear while standing behind me.

My body almost melted into oblivion by his tender tone in my ear while I leaned backward onto my locker. I lightly rubbed my hand up his chest toward his left cheek and caressed it with my palm. Right before I could say anything, I noticed Nate approaching us from down the hall. He smiled in approval of seeing his close friend showing interest in me. I snatched my hand away and brought it back to my side. My selfish thoughts, thinking of my future with Nate, did the best I could do in that moment.

"Oh em gee! You're so silly, Adam!" I busted out in an obnoxious giggle.

Adam's feet took a big step back. His face was squinted in confusion.

Nate took his final steps near us for a brief pause.

"What's going on with you guys?" Nate chuckled.

3

After Nate observed my near exposé of my relationship with Adam, he made a pivot around us to Crystal. We always managed to get lockers near each other since like sixth grade. He walked up to her slim frame and hunched down to embrace her.

"Hey-y-y, Nate," she seductively exhaled while wrapping her arms around his neck.

Their faces were cheek to cheek with their eyes closed. My stomach took twists in anger and hurt. My biggest desire was to get that same attention from him.

At night, I'd lay in bed and dream of getting a phone call or text from Nate. He would tell me how into me he is. I would tell him how much I like him too. After that, we would start dating and be the most popular and envied couple in school. Imagine that!

I feel like Crystal is prettier than me, which has made her more popular. It has also influenced Nate to give her more attention. She even has cute quirks about her that makes so many guys at school swoon.

One episode in the library…

"Like why are the books I need up so high?" Crystal whined in distress while stretching to reach above her head at the library.

One of the giant-sized basketball players laughed while grabbing the book for her.

"Here ya go, little lady!" he said, followed by biting his lip and passing her the large book from the top shelf.

"I could've gotten that myself, sir…if someone would've given me a boost," Crystal flirted back while prancing away with the textbook.

Male and female students nearby marveled at the cute flirty moment.

Maybe if Nate saw that, he would think differently about her hot-mess slutty act in front of all those people.

One weekend Crystal and Nate went to see some scary movie together. My heart ached at the thought of them being alone together. I could not go because I had to stay home with my little brother while my parents went out. The next day she called me. I asked her how the movie was. She told me how it scared her to the point that she slept with the lights on. I understood her feelings, but then she told me enough to know I needed to do some damage control.

"There was a part where they were driving and the killer came out of nowhere! I jumped so high and practically into Nate's arms to save me," Crystal girlishly whined on the phone.

She continued to ramble on about how much fun she was having with Nate. I only replied with "Oh, cool" in a fake enthusiasm. She did not catch on to my moody sarcasm. I was getting angrier and angrier while she boasted about her time spent with Nate. I wanted to tell her off and set this bitch straight about stepping on my toes and being with Nate when it's supposed to be me. Instead, I punched the wall in my bedroom.

"What was that noise?" Crystal asked, concerned about me.

I did not think she would hear my annoyed reaction to her constant bragging.

"I don't know. I think it was a car crash outside," I stuttered through my obvious lie.

It seemed like every day after school while walking home or over the weekend when we would hang out all she could talked about was Nate.

"Nate said this, Nate did that" was all I would hear from her. It was like she forgot how I saw him first. Nate and I are meant to be. One day he will confess his love for me in front of all of Hillman High. She just did not see it. He is using her to get to me. I know it. Why else would he hang out with her?

I repeatedly thought about how I could try a little bit harder for him to man up for me.

My inner thoughts: *I could maybe get a new hair sexy style or try some new makeup looks. That denim jacket that he complimented me on will make him notice me and refocus on the beginning of us as a couple. He had such a big smile on his face that day I wore it.*

"Hey, Mona, I like that jacket on you!" he said with a smile.

For the rest of the day, I had such a bright glow. I smiled at everyone, let a few people cut me in the lunch line, and even helped my mom do the dishes that night. He has had a real positive influence on me.

"See? I need him in my life. I will do whatever it takes for me and him to be able to start our relationship together," I told myself.

He just didn't see that Crystal was blocking our future...our love.

On a Friday night Josh Johnson had a house party.

Nate told me, "I hope to see you there," to which I flirted, "Only if you're going to be there."

I could tell our moment had arrived. He wanted me to be there with him one on one. I envisioned Nate putting his arm around me at the party, letting everyone know we were a thing. I even blushed at the thought of us standing alone in a corner and having a gentle first kiss.

Right after school that day I went to the mall and purchased dark-blue jeggings, an off-the-shoulder blouse, and even a new push-up bra. I had to be perfect for Nathan, my new boyfriend, on our first night being officially a couple.

Two hours before the party, Crystal texted me.

"Hey, do you want to ride together to Josh's later?"

I ignored her text. I am sure if I don't say I'm going, she won't go. Besides, I figured, I do not want her to feel hurt when Nathan announces his love for me in a party full of our classmates.

That night, at 10:00 p.m., I walked up to Josh's place. My feet could not help but to strut like I was on a New York City runway. I lightly finger combed my freshly blown-out hair and looked down at my outfit to make sure I still looked as flawless as when I left home. I rang the doorbell, and some random drunk guy answered.

"Ay-y-y-y, Mona's finally here…hey, Crystal and Nate are in the living room. I think I heard Adam was looking for you too," he announced over the loud music blaring through the house.

I heard the party status update while walking past him, but hearing Crystal and Nate were already there without me pissed me off.

"What the fuck was she thinking? What is she trying to do? She's literally trying too hard now!" I hissed to myself while navigating the house toward her.

The house was filled with students from school, dancing, laughing, talking, and drinking. I eventually found the living room and scanned through all the people until I found Crystal and Nate. They were cuddling and chatting with people sitting near them on the couch. My rage almost took over me, but I calmly walked over to the two.

"Hey, Crystal," I said, hugging her so that she'd have to pull away from Nate.

"I didn't hear from you, so I thought you were already here," Crystal said in worry.

"We have to talk!" I said in alarm.

I reached my hand out to which Crystal grabbed hold of and followed me back through the house and out the front door. It felt like we could not get to my home fast enough, and it was only a block away from Josh's. My main goal was to get her away from my man.

"Why are we running?" Crystal said, out of breath.

"We just need to hurry," I said while running in swift large steps.

The front yards flew by in my peripheral vision as we ran home. My focus was getting to my front door, getting inside, and confronting her.

Finally, after a five-minute sprint, we got to my place. I pondered on how to start the discussion. Gasping for air, I opened the front door and walked in. She followed. For a beat, I stood there staring at her, not sure of how to say what I needed without hurting her. My lips opened slightly, but nothing came out.

Breaking the silence, Crystal suggested, "Let's grab a snack and some water," as she walked to the kitchen.

I stood in the foyer unsure of what to say or do next for a moment, then I followed. I could hear the clanging of silverware and plates. Her pink manicured hands gripped the butcher knife, slowly slicing cheddar cheese from its block. I watched at how easy she could make things like this look.

"Grab us a plate behind you while I get the crackers…I know what calms you down when you're upset and needing some girl time," she said, certain about herself, laying the knife on the kitchen island's countertop.

My feet made a pivot to the cabinet behind me to get a single plate that we'd share.

"How about some saltines or multigrain crackers?" she asked while searching the pantry.

"Get the saltines…those are my fave," I called back.

She searched. I did not tell her we actually didn't have any more saltines. Her slim frame bobbed and weaved while looking high and low through the shelves of snacks, peanut butter, and pasta.

"I don't see it," she called over her shoulder.

My gaze scowled at the back of her head as she intently searched for the crackers. I thought, *She is never going to stop looking for the crackers just like how she is never going to stop chasing after Nate.*

I realized I needed to do the most drastic thing to keep Nate from getting caught up with Crystal. I grabbed the butcher knife on the counter and stepped swiftly toward Crystal

"How about another option?" she questioned.

"How about you stop chasing my man?" I quizzed back while fisting the black handle of the knife and underhandedly drove it into the middle of her back and stepped away.

"*Ah-h-h-h!*" Crystal screamed in disbelief, weakly turning to face me. "Why-y-y-y?" she cried while choking on the blood that came up through her mouth. She slumped over, knocking pantry items down, and dropped to her knees while I slowly reversed my footsteps. Tears welled under eyes as she lovingly reached toward me, asking me to save her. My body stood still, and my fingers released the knife. Her eyes stared, and her face seemed to accept its fate as she lay down and became still. I watched as her last breath exhaled from her body like the last drop of air from a helium-filled balloon.

My plan to just confront her did not work out as expected. My head nodded left to right as my feet walked over to her. I sat next to Crystal's bloody body the rest of that night. She got blood all over me, so I could not go back to the party. My shoulders shrugged up to my ears and released as I sighed in relief because Nate and I could be together without Crystal to distract either of us.

Some actions have unexpected aftermath though. I live in the county psych hospital. I am not sure if Nate knows to come here to see me or not. I miss him. I wonder if he is thinking of me.

This is my confession: I Mona Westly, killed my best friend, Crystal, in defense of love.

Mona uncrosses her legs, extends her limbs into a stretch, and closes her notebook. She tilts her head up to gaze at the moon shining down on her through the small window. Her body turns to tuck the notebook under the right side of her pillow. She lowers her body to the bed while memories of Crystal echo through her mind as she lays.

"Adam is cute. I think I'm going to love high school."

"Hey, do you want to ride together to Josh's later?"

"Why-y-y-y?"

The First Time

"I can't believe you've never done this before," Alyse said as the bedroom door swung open. Her buxom body sashayed into the room and looked back at her counterpart. The wind from the door swinging ajar and her head turn caused her chin-length bob to sway in the passing gust.

"Well, I guess there's a first time for everything," Steven replied, in his steps behind her.

While standing on the carpeted floor, she lifted her left foot and gripped her black high heel bootie off with her right hand. She did the same to her right shoe after. Her hourglass frame plopped and lay on the nearby bed. Her right hand patted the peach-colored comforter to invite her guest to join.

Steven stood motionless, watching in awe, but snapped out of his gaze after the almond-eyed beauty summoned his company at her side. His feet quickly stepped to the opposite end of the bed. He followed suit and slid off his oxfords one by one. He angled his khaki-covered rump next to the sultry femme and laid his giant physique backside down. Steven lay like an awkward unsure corpse.

"Why are you so uptight?" She chuckled.

"You're my long-time friend. I can't even believe you offered to do this for me," Steven said in an exhale. His eyes stared straight above at the white antique chandelier.

Alyse's body moved closer in a sultry slither. "So let me see what you got," she requested.

Steven's hands scrambled over his belt buckle to release its hold. Alyse, focused on the deed with her head down, angled her body over his lower half on all fours. Her head rose from watching his hustled hand motions to catching a mutual gaze with Steven's light-brown eyes. Her hand sensually swept her side bangs toward her temple, then the strands fell back over her right eye. Her bottom lip pulled into her mouth, and her teeth lightly grabbed hold but slowly let go afterward.

"Oh, is that your flashlight?" She giggled while taking control and pulling his pants down to his knees.

His navy-blue boxer briefs fit snuggly over his athletic waist, quads, and noticeable shaft.

"Ah, funny!" he replied with sarcastic amusement.

"My bad. Let us get this over with. Okay?" she indulged.

"Yes...let's..." He breathed out.

Her hands pinched his elastic waistband to lower it to the flat area above his member and aimed her face closer to get acquainted.

"This better not hurt," he warned.

Alyse's eyes rolled as she shook her head. In a dainty maneuver, she reached toward her side, squeezed her index finger and thumb into the front pocket of her fitted dark-indigo denim jean and slipped out a two-prong metal tool.

"Calm down, it's just an ingrown hair," she hissed as she angled the silver tweezers toward his fuzzy groin.

It's Too Late to Say "I Love You"

A dreary icy Saturday spotlights a bitter chill on a suburban Cape Cod cottage. The two-bedroom house homes a family that was once five, including a dog, but now holds four.

A five-feet-five coily hazelnut-haired girl lays face down on her twin-sized bed. Her cheek lays flush on her lush white comforter. The opposite side of the room has a fully made daybed adorned with cushy pillows all around. On the contrary, it looks welcoming but has a hint of cold, unwelcoming air.

I don't miss my sister since she went away, Alyssa thinks to herself.

Her mind continues to ponder. *I get time to be the only child now. It was annoying to always be compared to her.*

"Alyssa, you're late getting ready for school again!" my mom would say.

"Why can't you move faster or wake up earlier like your sister?" she'd scold.

It's easy to not miss my sister. At night she'd giggle and smile on her phone at funny memes from her friends…and cute texts from her boyfriend. I'd lay in bed across the room watching her live life to the fullest while my phone felt cold and lonely with no one to even like one of my selfie posts.

I got eighty likes in one hour once, but it was a photo of both of us sisters. We had an adventurous day touring her new college campus that day. She introduced me as "Alyssa, her little sis." I was proud of the title, especially since she finally stopped calling me her "baby sis."

After that weekend touring her new school, I thought of how much I was going to miss her while she was away, but then she "borrowed" my yoga mat and didn't put it back in its normal spot, leaving me to scramble at the last minute for my session. She thought it was funny that I was late to get my "Zen on" and laughed while driving me to my yoga-Pilates class. I was angry. So I went back to anticipating her time away at college in the fall.

By the end of summer, she was preparing for her new journey in life.

"Don't forget to write!" I joked repeatedly while helping her pack.

"I'm excited for college, but…what are you going to do without me?" she somberly replied after my third jest.

"Oh, I'll be *fine!*" I enthusiastically exclaimed.

"But who's going to pick you up from school? Or help you with homework? Or look out for you?" she quizzed.

"Oh, don't you worry your pretty ole heart now…you git on outta here," I continued to jeer.

This week my parents and I had Thanksgiving dinner. Her usual seat sat hollow and anticipating her goofy giggles, sarcastic smiles, and obnoxious chewing. Most college students are home this time of year with their families. When I wished to be an only child, I did not wish for it to be at the hands of a drunk driver. Now I wish I could tell my sister I miss and love her.

A Request from a Stranger

A scorching September Saturday in 1997. There's rowdy cheering and laughter of children running and hopping around outside and metal squeaking of the playground equipment wafting into a third-floor apartment window of an East Harlem tower.

"You are very pretty," Babs blurts in a high pitch. "You remind me of my younger self." She sheepishly chuckles.

She forces her golden-brown hands into a prim fold on her lap with her back upright in a stiff hold to mirror her caramel-toned guest.

"I'll take that as a compliment," Ella replies with an obligated smile and nod. She refrains an expression of disgust that questioned Babs's gray tooth revealing itself from the right side of her smile. Instead, she openly glances around the room. Her eyes lead her head in turns and lifts while examining her surroundings. "How long have you lived here?" Ella asks.

"About twenty-seven years now," Babs replies eagerly while nodding her head up and down. "Since right afta you was born."

The conversation pauses into an ear-aching silence.

The two women sit on opposing sides of the taupe-walled room. It is filled with a broken brown-and-black corduroy couch, square mahogany coffee table, and the two tufted Parson's chairs where they are seated. A nectarine-toned haze spotlights a corner of the ceiling from a table lamp's shade. The household vacuum seems to be missing in action based on the appearance of the rundown dusty carpet.

Boiling from the smothering heat, Ella uses her right-hand index finger and thumb to pinch a black-coated elastic off her left wrist. After it has been removed, she lifts her hands to scoop her long, coarse, curly jet-black hair into a high bun. It sits like a disheveled crown with random ringlets springing from her temples.

"The air conditioning should start cooling the room off soon," Babs says in an adoring observation. "I always knew you was gon have a head full of long hair, Ellie." She smiles.

"It's El-la," Ella snaps with an exaggerated enunciation. "No one has called me that since I was a baby." She glares back at Babs.

"I named you Ella after my mother," Babs says tenderly. "My family called you Ellie to tell between the two of yous."

Ella stares emotionless at Babs.

"Baby Ellie!" Babs continues. "That's what your aunts, uncles, and cousins would say when dey come ova to see you."

Ella's frown turns to a slight delighted grimace.

"But you got a nice upbringing with your Irish father and..." Babs pauses in deep thought. "I'm sure Valentina let you think you was a Dominican like her all these years. I couldn't be a rich housewife like your father wanted, but I always wanted you in my life."

Ella releases her tense shoulders with an audible outward breath.

"I'm sorry, sweetie," Babs softly responds. "I figured, you were here to learn 'bout your past. Do you want to know where you came from? How you got dat scar on your left arm?" She points toward Ella's left side while holding gaze.

"My mother told me I was an active baby and didn't sit still while she held me, and the doctor gave me my shot," Ella explains knowingly.

"Yes, me, yamotha, took you to the doctah," Babs corrects proudly. "Yo daddy would call me and ask 'bout you…I told him dat story."

Silence swarms into the room while the two women stare at each other. Their blinking eyes are the only movement as the room cools off.

"Your father," Babs starts to break the silence, "he ain't want no stripper raising his baby…hell, he ain't want no black stripper to be his baby's mama." She chuckles.

Ella continues to listen.

"It doesn't matter to me that you're here to request my help for your blood transfusion." Babs stifles on a tear. "I gave you all I got in the beginning, and I'll give you all that I have in me to make sure you continue to live your life."

"I am…just in a world of shock. Disbelief. I thought I knew myself… and where I came from *already*." Ella chokes on a sob and holds it in. A shallow well forms under each eye.

Babs makes a quick step across the room with both hands extended toward Ella.

"I never wanted you to find out this way," Babs says while clutching Ella in her arms. "But it feels so good to be holding you now."

"I thought…," Ella sobs, "I thought…I just…don't understand…to find out that the woman who raised me…she lied…she's not my mother… I feel incomplete."

A Mother's Day Tale

Daylight beams through a bay window as it frames the view of the backyard of its neighboring home. Near the windowsill, Doris, a middle-aged blonde sits sideways, hugging her knees to her chest while scowling at the children playing. She tucks her shoulder-length hair behind her ears, then rewraps her arms around her bent legs. Her mind wanders as she analyzes the kids.

"Hmmph, that little Mia is getting darker and darker as she plays in the sun. Don't those Johnsons know to put sunblock on *that* child?"

Five-year-old Mia resembles the light-caramel-toned singer Alicia Keys but with light hair and light-brown eyes.

Doris's head shakes disappointingly.

"Tah! She is just full of joy playing with her older black brothers and sisters like they all belong together…like they belong in this neighborhood. Ha! Those kids…and their fake lawyer parents…"

Her lips frown as if she smells a rancid stench while her head nods side to side.

"They throw backyard parties and blasting that hip-hop music."

Her expression changes to cheerful as she thinks of her offspring.

"*My* Bethany has gone on to graduate school with an amazing life ahead of her. She's come a long way, and I'm so proud of her. Why, my darling already has a promising job lined up in New York City. I am so glad she has made good decisions. She ended that relationship with that ole Jamaal and took an internship. Her life's choices were even better with my guidance, I am sure. It will be a true delight when my Bethany comes home this weekend. She usually comes home with flowers and a balloon that says, 'Happy Mother's Day!'"

Doris smiles while stuck in deep thought.

"Last year Mia and her siblings gave their mother, Mrs. Johnson, a gold necklace to celebrate her. She is a good mom, I guess."

Doris releases a huff as she disappointingly admits to Mrs. Johnson being a good parent.

"While Mrs. Johnson was busy being so delighted with her new jewelry, she sent the kids over that Sunday afternoon with cookies to say, 'Happy Mother's Day!' It was thoughtful of them."

Her face turns to a grimace.

"The kids don't like me. They think I'm the mean old lady next door. So, of course, they did not want to even say hi to me, let alone show up at my front door to wish me a 'Happy Mother's Day.'"

Doris reflects on the last Mother's Day.

"Happy Mother's Day, Mrs. Smith!" the older kids said in unison while Mia chimed in delayed with their practiced announcement.

The oldest boy handed me a tray of cookies, but I couldn't stop eyeing Mia. I could feel her honey-brown gaze see into my core. Time stood still as I admired her silky coiled caramel hair and her chicklet- toothed smile.

"If only Bethany was older and settled in her life...she could have been a better mother to her half-breed baby, sweet Mia."

Good Ole Gladys

Gladys, a plump brunette with gray streaks in her hair, lays strewn across a navy-blue chaise lounge. The sun gradually rises and blankets her pale skin as she slowly awakens.

"Where the hell am I?" she announces in a boozed daze.

A slim caramel-toned woman gleefully prances from her bedroom through her open-concept home. Her shoulder-length raven-colored ringlets bounce with her walk as she smiles from inner thoughts. Her sashay skips a beat when she reaches the living room leading to the kitchen.

"Oh, you're awake," Donna replies to the disappointing image.

"Excuse me," Gladys calls to Donna. "Ma'am, I didn't have a chocolate on my pillow last night."

"You're lucky I gave you a pillow," Donna remarks snidely.

She places a K-Cup in the coffee brew machine and presses the start button. Gladys lifts her head to get a view of Donna.

"I used to look like you." Gladys smiles. Her ear-to-ear grin reveals missing teeth on the right side of her mouth.

"And then what?" Donna requests.

Gladys chuckles. "And then nothing. I guess that's not a compliment since I'm old and fat now…aye."

Donna sips her steaming coffee and stares blankly at her house guest.

"Okay, I'd look like you if I was dark…like you have tan skin and I'm white," Gladys further explains her case.

Donna swiftly stomps to the living room area, snatches up the black duffel bag from the floor near the chaise lounge. She returns to the kitchen and grabs a few items from the pantry, tossing them into the bag.

"Now, now, sweetie. I don't mean any harm. My dead husband Harvey was black," Gladys continues while watching Donna quickly travel from room to room of the two-thousand-square-foot ranch.

"He left us…and then he died."

"*Mom*! So stop reminiscing like he was this great man," Donna sneers. She hands Gladys the duffle bag.

Gladys slowly stands from her seat, squinting her eyes in confusion. She ignores Donna's anger. "You do look like you could be my daughter, but she's a little girl. Only seven years old with nappy curly pigtails." She groans from elderly pains as she stands from her seat.

"You have to stop these antics." Donna sighs as a tear rolls down her right cheek. "Next time I find you drunk and passed out on the sidewalk, I'm leaving you there."

Accepting the filled bag and walking toward the front door, Gladys declares, "This is a rude bed and breakfast."

"Your ride back to the home will be here in two minutes," Donna says over her left shoulder while walking toward her bedroom. The door closes behind her.

"That lady reminds me of my baby girl Donna. I sure do miss her," Gladys thinks out loud.

Death to Ms. Valentine

A shiny white casket presents a butterscotch-tinted female figure while somber chapel music plays. She lays at peace while the waves of her chestnut-colored hair flow past her shoulders almost endlessly. Her husband, Troy, and her best friend, Olivia, stood nearby observing the lifeless shell that used to be Val.

"I can't believe this is real," Olivia whispers to Troy.

"Me either," he replies. "I miss her so much." He chokes on a sob and cups his hand over his mouth.

*****

Inaudible, Val's agonized soul explodes like a grenade, rattling through her bombshell frame.

"*What* the *fuck* happened *here*? I am not supposed to be dead right now! I am supposed to be burying Troy right now and living happily ever after—dating boy toys and going on shopping sprees. Ar-r-r-g-g-g-h-h-h!"

"I'm too gorgeous to die...and who the fuck asked for daisies! Troy knows I only prefer red roses. Damn it! His cheap ass probably tried to save money. Even in my death he is penny-pinching. He probably ordered carnations, but Olivia made him spend the extra few dollars. Liv, hmmm, my fave car mechanic turned bestie always looks out for me. As for Troy, I...bet...he...asked one of his boys to drive us all to the burial site in his old clunker Expedition. I can't even die as the princess I've always been. Wahh!"

Val's body permanently rests, but her soul is sleepless and rationalizing.

"I don't get it. How did my plan with Olivia fail?"

Val reflects on what led her to this rigor mortis.

Two weeks ago.

"So tomorrow night," Val whispers on the phone, "I'll go to do my usual grocery store trip around seven thirty…"

"And I will call the house telling Troy there's been an accident and for him to come right away," Olivia adds in.

"Yes, but make sure to stop by as soon as it gets dark to cut the brake line on the BMW, the black car," Val instructs.

Back in her casket, Val is confident in her plan, but it failed unfortunately.

"I'm sure Olivia did it correctly."

*****

Troy and Liv admire in a daze on the dearly departed Val.

"I miss my wife so much," Troy whimpers.

He turns and bends at his waist toward Olivia. She quickly reaches up toward his shoulders to embrace him.

"Do you know what happened to her?" Olivia asks in a low murmur.

"Something about her brakes in her white Mercedes gave out," Troy whispers back with a confused frown.

"And your car, the black BMW is okay. Right?" she asks.

"No problems," he blurts in between his whimpers.

"Oh," she replies in a sullen tone.

Olivia continues her squeeze on Troy and gazes up to the sunlight showing through the stained-glass window. It spotlights onto the casket as Olivia's eyes glisten in a bright beam, and her frown turns to a delightedly sly grin. Val's demise is Olivia's prize.

Oblivious

A glossy dark-haired femme sits cross-legged in her navy-blue Egyptian-cotton-dressed king bed. Her coral-gel-manicured fingers hold her smartphone to her right ear. Her head tilts back on the tan-colored tufted headboard behind her. She gleefully chats with her supportive mother.

"This romantic weekend away for Christmas was *all* his idea…" Lena says, then pauses to listen to her mother's reply. Her eyes stare into the ceiling in a dreamy daze while listening on the call.

"*Yes!* I can tell, Mom," she says reassuringly. "My ring is coming. I always knew he was the one." She sighs in relief.

The pleasant ping of another call chimes through.

"Speaking of—" She cuts off her mother's sentence. "He's on the other line. Call you later, Mom. Love you," she says before switching lines to answer the other call.

"Hey," his voice says in a rushed monotone.

"Hi, ba-a-a—" Lena gleams until she is cut off.

"How are you?" he abruptly ends her sentence.

"I am great! But, uhh, so-o-o when should I be ready for our weekend away?" her excitement divulges.

"Well, uhm, that's what I was calling to say...," he slowly states.

Her pink-glossed smile turns to a frown.

"That may not be happening," he spews out.

Her heart hammers through her chest to release from its agony.

"But you promised! Especially since you didn't even get to meet my family on Thanksgiving," she pleas.

"I know, I know," he says.

"I have another surprise for you though...N-New Y-Year's. N-New Year's Eve is going to be great for us!" He delivers in an upbeat stutter.

"Oh-h-h-h-h," an exhausted sigh releases from her mouth. "So I have to wait another month to be with you?" Her eyes squint and scan the room while searching her thoughts.

"Listen, don't be upset. I just have a lot with work and my mom," he insists.

"This is not a real relationship!" Lena's voice raises. "I haven't even met your friends or family..."

"*You will!*" he yells. "You will, baby...soon." His voice lowers to calm the brewing storm.

She hears the creaking of a door squeak open, then closed in the distance behind him.

"Hi, honey, the business trip got cancelled," a mature womanly voice announces after her entrance into the room he's seated in.

The sound of steady high heel taps gets louder as they near him.

"Hi, baby!" he replies to this mysterious figure, followed by the smack of a lip-to-lip kiss.

"Umm, hello?" Lena says, confused and almost speechless by the realization.

"Oh yeah, so, Rob, I'll call you later. My fiancée just got home," his cheerful voice declares before ending the call.

"Wait! What? *Rob*…are you kidding, asshole?" rolls off her tongue.

The call ends before the last of her words are audible.

"I don't believe this *shit!*" She pouts while eyeing her prepacked silver upright suitcase.

Her legs unravel and swing to hit the floor. She digs her index finger and thumb into her mouth to take out her dental retainer and place it in the blue plastic case on her nightstand. Her feet scamper across the room to grab a worn pair of jeans and pink sweatshirt on the walk-in closet floor.

"This bitch thinks she can step in and ruin my life!" she screams. "*Who the hell does she think she is?*" Lena ferociously grunts while stumbling to quickly get dressed.

As she walks from the bedroom, through the hall, to the small cottage's front door, her angry foot thumps cause the fish residing in the narrow throughway to jostle around.

I love him. I can't lose him, she thinks. *When the hell did he get engaged?*

Her right hand reaches forward, turns the gold knob, and…her feet are unexpectedly glued to the cherry wood floor.

"No," she tells herself softly.

Her eyes shut into a tight squeeze. Wells of water form under each eye as she closes the door and pivots back to her bedroom. The droplets scorch down her face while she slowly treads back to her bedroom. Her jeans followed by her sweatshirt are removed from her slim frame in a slothful manner when she reaches her bed. They lay inside-out on the floor near where she stands. Half-dressed, she plops on the bed face first while her wailing is muffled by the pillows surrounding her.

Bing, bong, bing. Lena's smartphone cheerfully chimes in the back pocket of her jeans on the hardwood floor.

The simultaneous vibrating and ring make her pause and roll her body toward the music coming from her gadget. Her right arm dangles over the side of the bed and snatches the phone from the floor. The screen reads "Jonathan" while continuing to scream and shake its alert in her hand. She stares at the screen, wipes a tear, and places the phone on the nearby nightstand.

Seconds later the chiming and shaking starts again.

Bing, bong, bing, bing, bong… It tries to tempt her.

But it rings and rings…

Modern-Day Cat Lady

Standing in her dimly lit bedroom, Wanda, an average-height creamy-caramel-toned dame with straight raven-colored hair admires herself in the mirror. She is wearing a navy-blue lace camisole with matching boy-short panties.

Full-grown male cats roam her bedroom while she flips her hair and makes sexy pout facial expressions before snapping photos of her reflection.

"You're a freakin' vixen, you gorgeous cat lady you," says Wanda's twin from the mirror admiringly.

The camera light on her smartphone clicks as brightness bounces off the mirror. The twin vamps flirtatiously marvel at each other.

"Spinsters are never this hot," she compliments back.

Dexter, one of the cats, leaps off the nightstand and rubs his head on her toned shin after he reaches the floor. Wanda slowly arches her back as she leans forward at her waist to pat and rub her dark-gray feline.

"I'm so happy to still have you in my life, Dex." She grins. "I. Have. Seven. Cats," she says delightedly while scanning the room and glancing at each male feline.

The lookalikes take a long pause.

Wanda snaps out of it after a beat.

Standing, she lifts her body at its highest with the balls of her feet and twirls one round on her big toes. She releases and lowers her slim-curvy frame in a ballerina's graceful flow. Her twin still holds gaze and watches, aroused by the pleasurable sight.

Wanda pauses after her pirouette and seductively smirks back at her twin.

"You're right. I'm a hot-ass cat lady." She chuckles.

Her twin's lips move from pursed tight to a reassuring smile and up-down nod.

"I've been called so many hurtful things as a woman—whore, slut, thot—never a sexy single bachelorette." She rolls her eyes while speaking to her reflection.

Her smile turns grim. "I'm having so much fun…no, I'm not-t-t!" she outbursts as water fills like wells in her lower eyelids.

Her twin rolls her dark eyes upward while crossing her arms in front of her chest and nodding her head.

"Snap out of it," her twin demands.

"I *do* have *my* cats!" she protests. Wanda takes a deep breath in, causing her shoulders to rise followed by a loud sigh.

Her twin does the same.

She grimaces with a slight giggle while her twin stares, confused by Wanda's lame humor.

"For the last seven years I've brought a new guy to family gatherings. He attends the Halloween party, Thanksgiving dinner, and even the Christmas Eve and Christmas Day family vacation…"

Her half-dressed body plops sideways on her bed, angling, so that she can still admire her Coke-bottle figure. She props her head up with her bent right arm, then tucks her hair behind her left ear. Her eyes keep contact with her image in the gold-framed mirror.

"Then, like clockwork, right before New Year's Day, my new suitor tells me he's leaving me. I do everything to keep him. I cook. I clean. I give more affection. My visual pain won't even convince him to stay," she whines.

The well underneath her right eye releases a steamy droplet down her cheek toward her jawline. A daze takes over her, and she's silent.

Leo, her ginger-colored feline leaps on the California king-sized bed and slowly saunters his way over to her, causing her daze to end.

"Then I use my sultry craft to keep them from leaving me." She smirks.

Her left hand reaches toward the cat to caress his back. He collapses next to her, indulging into her touch.

"And now we're all living happily ever after, right, boys?"

"Me-e-e-o-w-w-w," the cats all wail in unison.

Trikk Queen

It has been five months since I paid off my luxury condo with a view of the New York City skyline.

Two months ago, I sent my parents on a month-long vacation to Jamaica on my "lottery winnings."

Last week, I hired a personal assistant who runs my errands, pays my bills, walks my dog, and sends slutty texts on my behalf to my lovers when I am busy.

Before you assume that I am a lazy pyramid-scheme running escort, just know that I believe I have helped people control their substance abuse.

My rise to wealth started three years ago as a prank. I decided to get my coworker/bestie, Chrissy, *high* to loosen her up at the company's holiday party. After all the financial reports she organized and presented to our VPs, she deserved to have some fun. So after her small chat with her office crush turned sour, I walked her to the restroom.

Awkward discomfort showed in her doe-like eyes. Hoping to ease the pain, I reached into my clutch with my index finger and thumb to reveal a tiny clear vial with a black cap filled with (pause)…let us call it a white powdery substance.

"I don't know about this…" Chrissy nodded.

Disregarding her comment, I poured the substance onto the scoop part of my pinky fingernail. I could only base my actions on what I have seen on TV.

"Can I get in on that?"

A familiar voice requested from a distance about three stalls away.

Chrissy tilted her head, extending her neck to see over my shoulder, and I turned slightly to see where the request is coming from.

I hesitated. "Get in on *this*?" I replied like an amateur.

The last stall door swung open, revealing my director, Janis. Her dark sultry and intrigued eyes held gaze with me as her footsteps came closer to us.

"I really need to get through this dull night," Janis said suavely when she reached our standing point of the bathroom.

I passed her the vial, and she sprinkled a tiny hit on the back of her left hand. We watched in awe as she brought her diamond-dressed wrist closer to her face, held her right nostril closed with her right hand, and vacuumed the dust up her left nostril.

"Ah-h-h-h," Janis sighed and fluttered her lashes. "Come, have a drink with me before you girls leave." Janis checked her reflection, pinched her nose to grab the white excess, and rubbed her fingers together until the powder disintegrated. Her slim figure swiftly glided out of the bathroom along with the taps of her four-inch-high pumps.

"Your turn." I gestured the vial at Chrissy for her to give me her hand.

Reluctantly, she followed Janis's same steps, but her attempt to be suave turned to uncontrollable flinching and coughing.

"This better make me a rich bitch like Janis too." Chrissy coughed.

I followed suit and could not help to cough, flinch, and flicker my eyes as well. I was shocked by the sense of clarity my mind felt ten minutes later. I could not believe I cooked up a potion that had *this effect*.

Seeing it as a networking opportunity, we made our way to the corner of the bar Janis was standing at and chatting up one of the hottest guys from the office. My mental plan was to chat and have a few shots with Janis before the night ended.

"There you ladies are." Janis smiled. "I was just telling Adam about how much fun you two ladies are."

Without hesitation, Adam asked in a flirty charismatic tone, "Would you ladies care to share?"

The glisten in his eyes seduced my soul, but I played nonchalant. I swung my hand forward. "It's so nice to meet you." I smiled. "I think I've seen you around before."

We shook hands with the vial transferring from my hand to his. He grinned, then walked away.

Chrissy got the sense of courage she needed at the party. We effortlessly chatted up a few VPs and laughed about our night on the way home. I felt like a proud mom watching my girl passed out on my couch.

"I can't believe how friendly and flirty you were with Adam." Chrissy laughed. "I admired how cool you played it off," she continued.

"I almost wet my pants when our fingers touched." I smirked.

Next workday my list of besties in the office had grown. Janis seemed to spread the word about me. VPs, directors, and even the CEO, knew my name not only because of my hard work in the office, but also for my overnight sensation of a side hustle. They assumed I worked for a man, but I was my own boss.

I had weekly private meetings with the CEO to discuss "deliveries."

"Stella, your boss makes an amazing hit!" he spoke in a low tone while shaking my hand. "Last batch caused me to wake up not knowing where the f@#k I was." He chuckled.

I chuckled too. I was in disbelief of the luck I had come across.

People in the office hate me for my popularity. I, of course, love the attention and do my best to ignore the haters anyway.

I have heard whispers from random coworkers as I walk by.

"It's like she's got some kind of hold on them."

Many do not know why management plays favorites with me. It is a simple formula: three parts baking soda, two parts crushed baby aspirin. Harmless fun combined with *legal* substances. I am not hurting anyone, just fulfilling a demand.

In a Memento

Day 67

A gray midday spotlights on a rectangular windowpane. Water spills onto the dusty glass as if to clean the filth that lingers on the other side.

A frail petite frame is lying on a twin-sized bed. Slowly, she extends her arms and legs in opposing directions, awakening her senses while freeing her emerald eyes from their lids.

"Ahhh," releases from her widely parted lips as she sits up and drapes her legs over the side of the bed.

"Oh shit! Where's my phone?"

She sends her hands flailing to hunt through the white snack-stained sheets.

"Got it!" She holds it to the sky as if it is a trophy.

Her feet race to the bathroom located through a white wooden door connected to the bedroom. She wiggled her hips and inserted her thumbs behind her elastic waistband to guide her shorts down her legs. Her sleep shorts are at her ankles. Morinne's elbows are resting on her knees at a forty-five-degree angle while she taps away on the touch screen of her smartphone.

"He-he-he-he…group chat was crazy last night."

This is the happiness she lives for.

"Oh, aww." Her head tilts to the right with a lovestruck grin. "Drew-w-w-w! He said, 'Good morning, beautiful.' I hope he's coming by later." Her smile holds for a beat, then she snaps out of her daze.

"Let's get the day started." Her feet steady to the floor before her legs straighten and lead her back into the bedroom.

Maureen's throne hisses behind her, then fades to silence while she plops onto the unmade sheets. She reaches her right hand toward her head, scratching her scalp lightly to not disturb the messy nest held by a skinny elastic on top. Her twig of an arm points forward, holding a slim silver remote.

"I can't wait to catch up on Netflix," she announces as the TV chimes on.

Day 210

A golden midday spotlights onto a rectangular windowpane. The sun gleams through the dusty glass as if to overpower the gray filth.

A frail petite frame is lying on a twin-sized bed. Slowly, she extends her arms and legs in opposing directions, awakening her senses while freeing her eyes from their lids.

"Ahhh," releases from her widely parted lips as she sits up and drapes her legs over the side of the bed.

"Oh shit! Where's my phone?"

She sends her hands flailing to hunt through the white snack-stained sheets.

"Got it!" She holds it to the sky as if it is a trophy.

Her feet race to the bathroom located through a white wooden door in the bedroom. She wiggled her hips and inserted her thumbs behind her elastic waistband to guide her shorts down her legs. Her sleep shorts are at her ankles. Morinne's elbows are resting on her knees at a forty-five-degree angle while she taps away on the touch screen of her smartphone.

"He-he-he-he…group chat was crazy last night."

This is the happiness she lives for.

"Oh, aww." Her head tilts to the right with a lovestruck grin. "Drew-w-w! He said, 'Good morning, beautiful.' I hope he's coming by later." Her smile holds for a beat, then snaps out of her daze.

"Let's get the day started." Her feet steady to the floor before her legs straighten and lead her back into the bedroom.

Maureen's throne hisses behind her, then fades to silence while she plops onto the unmade sheets. She reaches her right hand toward her head, scratching her scalp lightly to not disturb the messy nest held by a skinny elastic on top. Her twig of an arm points forward, holding a slim silver remote.

"I can't wait to catch up on Netflix," she announces as the television chimes on.

Outside her door

Sandra and Patty are curiously peering through the square-shaped window in Maureen's locked door.

"She seems harmless. Poor girl," Sandra says.

"Hmmmph, not really." Patty snickers.

"Oh, come on, I heard she had a six-figure job, luxury apartment, and handsome fiancé before ending up here."

"Yeah, and thanks to *catching* her handsome fiancé with another woman…Poor girl." Patty nods her head left to right. "She had a nervous breakdown and couldn't function."

Sandra stares observantly at the patient with pity in her eyes.

"She taps on a disconnected smartphone and watches movies on VHS all day," Patty says before a long pause. "I wouldn't want a man so handsome to ruin my life, causing insanity to become my eternity." She adds, "They. Never. Found. The. Body." She nods with every syllable to Sandra.

The two women swivel their hips, pivot from the door, and stroll away in unison.

Day 376

A blue midday spotlights on an upright rectangular pane. Fluffy flakes dance outside the dusty glass as if taunting the filth that lingers on the other side.

A frail petite frame is lying on a twin-sized bed. Slowly, she extends her arms and legs in opposing directions, awakening her senses while freeing her emerald eyes from their lids.

"Ah…"

Just Being a Good Friend

"I just don't know how we ended up here," Cassandra says.

We sit at opposite ends of my sky-blue couch. Tears well up under her jade-toned eyes. My heart aches for my neighbor turned best friend.

"Maybe you two can try therapy again," I reply sincerely with a slight shrug.

"Yeah, maybe...," she says while tucking her strawberry-brownish hair behind her left ear.

"Well, listen, you can stay in our guest room for as long as you want... my husband will be away at work for a few days anyway," I try to console.

"I'd hate to inconvenience you, Lorna," she says.

Cassandra crosses her yoga-toned legs, then brings her knees to her chest and wraps her cardigan tightly around her frame like a security blanket. The fetus-shaped ball she has curled into is like an invisible bubble blown to protect her heart from any more pain. While watching her, my head tilts to the right as I think, *I want to cure her pain.*

"It's no inconvenience, Cass. I'd love the company," I reassure.

Three years ago, Cass and Mark moved in next door. It was a breath of fresh air to have her in my life. We went from "Welcome to the neighborhood" to "We should go workout" and eventually "How about a girl's night out?"

To see Cass in pain hurts me to the core. Hearing that Mark has been cheating on her makes me wonder how blind and dumb he is.

"How about some hot tea?"

"Yeah, sure." She sniffles.

I stand and sashay my broad pear-shaped hips toward the kitchen sink, then turn to watch her from the open-floor planned layout.

"Peppermint tea, okay?" I call over to her.

"Yeah, that's fine," she announces back while nodding and blowing her nose into a facial tissue.

I grab the kettle on the stove and pivot to face the sink. My right hand lifts the faucet lever to release water into the red teapot.

My mind cannot help but to find itself in a daze. I reminisce about the first time I saw the slim-toned yogi practicing her tree pose while her flowy ponytail lightly dusted across her ballerina-postured shoulders. I was sipping a new-flavored coffee while seated at the breakfast bar and admiring her as she practiced in her backyard. The morning brew warmed my soul, and her presence heated a desire in me. Such a sweet soul should be given all the world has to offer, not pain.

Mark does not deserve her. He cannot love her the way I know I can. Right now, is not a good time to share these thoughts with her though.

I snapped out of my daze to carry on hosting.

"I sprinkled in raw sugar for you…" My bare feet slap the hard wood floor while carrying the hot mugs to the living room area to accompany my friend in need.

Transformation

A five-feet-ten shirtless muscular male is slowly pacing through a dark kitchen while holding a smartphone to his ear. He stops in his track in front of the window above the sink, tilts his head back, and lightly closes his eyes as the lamppost outside reveals his arched brows, chiseled jaw, and enticingly plump lips. He lets out a silent sigh.

"I know, baby," he says. "Yes, yes…I will not be late tomorrow. No worr—"

The muffled sound of a female's voice pouting filters through the phone causes him to pause.

"This doctor is one of the best, baby! I'm so excited, but I want to make a good impression…you know, for our bastard child," she says.

"No worries," he replies to assure her.

Female voice continues, "I wonder if I'll still be pregnant on our wedding day or if you'll wait to propose after the baby is born. You know our child deserves—"

"Hey, my love, please go get your rest…tomorrow is a big day for us. I love you," he cuts her off.

"Yes, okay, baby. I love you too. Good night." She sniffles.

He looks down at the smartphone in the palm of his hand, places his thumb on the red button to end the call, and lays the phone on the kitchen counter he is standing next to.

"Aaaargh!" he groans while lacing his fingers through his messy cropped haircut. Shaking his head left to right in disbelief, he walks through the dark warehouse loft to the living room area. His body plops on the dark-chocolate leather couch face up. His eyes stare at the ceiling as if searching for an answer. He starts to spew his feelings out loud.

"I cannot believe she would do this to me! The woman of my dreams is lying to me! Faaawck! I mean, no one is perfect, but it took me most of my life to get to where I am. Hmmph, seven years ago she would not have wanted me. But *now* I have a vacation home in Belize, townhome in LA, a digital marketing firm, amazing abs, and I'm a new *man*! This bitch wants to take me for all I've got.

"I know what my problem is, the sex is too good." He slyly smirks. "But Billie Jean won't be framing me, hmmph. I'm 100 percent sure I'm not the father. Ha! Ha!" He impersonates Maury Povich's voice. "She would have a fit if I told her I got a vasectomy or something. Nah! I can't keep lying to her. Would she forgive my actual truth? I don't want to scare her off and…I don't want to lose her. I did always want to be a parent. Do I want to knowingly raise another man's child? Some baby-making man's child…or should I keep my mouth shut because she does want to be with me." He wraps his arms to hug himself. "I've come a long way since I was a confused woman waiting for her operation."

Fighting the Setbacks

5:00 a. m.

A rectangular-shaped digital alarm clock beeps obnoxiously.

A voluptuous body connected to a chipmunk-faced lady turns her head toward her left shoulder to view the morning. She glares at the beige curtain-dressed window. The morning is hazy and dim. Rolling her eyes, she extends her right arm at the night table next to her bed, swinging it to end the buzzer. Her index finger presses on the button to end the noise.

"Yah-h-h-h," she blurts out of her widely open mouth as she sits up to stretch her arms above her golden tussled tresses. She turns to look at her sleeping bedmate. "Babe…babe…," she whispers.

His white-shirted back faces her. He lays still and unbothered.

Her right hand reaches toward him and rubs his upper back. He still does not budge. She gives a light nudge after and stares, waiting for a reply.

"Yes, sweetie," he unconsciously mumbles.

"Don't forget to wake the kids and get them dressed. My CrossFit trainer is waiting to torture me into another intense workout." She giggles.

"Arrggh, alight," he says, yawning.

"And don't forget their oatmeal for breakfast. Their lunches are packed," she continues as her feet hit the floor.

Unenthused, "Yep!" he says while stretching. He rises from the bed and takes a deep breath.

Her feet scurry to the lounge chair posted in the corner of the room and strips herself of her white silk slip nightie.

"I'm serious. No more pastries or big slices of cake for breakfast. I don't want out kids to be obese," she scolds.

He walks over to his pretty plush bride and grabs her naked body with his long meaty arms. He mumbles into her neck, "I don't see a problem with that."

"Oh, come on. Really, babe! We've discussed this before." She girlishly laughs. "This will make me feel better. Plus, I want to look good for your sister's wedding this summer. No more Shamu standing behind the skinny chick in photos," she rants and wiggles to release from his hold.

She bends at her waist to grab floral-designed stretch pants and a white T-shirt. Her head inserts into the white top and pops through, dragging her straight-brown hair into a tousled mess. Her fingers grab the strands that linger under the shirt. Next, her feet insert one by one into the tight bright pants. Her wide hips and round rump swivel into the sweat-wicking tights.

"Well, I hope you and your aerobics teacher have a nice time pumping iron or whatever it is you do." He sighs while watching her walk away.

"Ha! Ha! It's cross-training Mr. Ex-High School Jock. Time has been catching up to you…and your beer belly." She smirks. In a quick swoop, she grabs the gym bag and water bottle waiting for her on the floor near the bedroom door.

He looks down at himself with both hands on his hips and a wide-legged stance. "I thought you liked my hairy gut," he jeers, then pats his stomach.

"I'll see you later. Love you," she announces. Her stride makes a beeline for the front door of their two-bedroom apartment.

Whispers and giggling stirs from the bedroom opposite the master suite.

"I love you too, baby," he replies.

Her hand reaches the gold doorknob and turns clockwise.

"Oh, babe, I forgot to tell you...," he obliges.

"Oh my gosh, babe. What is it?" She pauses in her tracks. Her feet pivot. When her body turns, her eyes hold an unblinking gaze with her husband.

"I forgot to tell you. Kevin is supposed to bring cookies for the bake sale," he continues. "Nothing store bought is allowed."

"Ah-h-h-h," she loudly sighs. "Call your mom. I'm out the door right now."

"Actually, Mom's knee is still bad. She can't stand for too long honey," he debates.

"I have to go, babe. You'll figure it out," she hisses.

The door swings open, and she steps one foot out of the door.

"We can't send Kevin to school without the cookies. We signed up for this," he disputes.

Her footsteps reverse through the threshold in a slow, deliberate manner. Her hands release the gym bag and water bottle onto the hardwood floor near the front entrance. In a huff, she walks into the kitchen, flips a light on, grabs eggs from the refrigerator, and places them on the kitchen island countertop. With a stoic expression, she glides to the pantry and reaches slightly overhead to nab a bag of white sugar off the top shelf.

He watches her attitude transition, then saunters away to walk back into the dark bedroom.

"Yeah, do your aerobics mess some other time." He smirks and mumbles.

"It's the same hamster wheel to nowhere every day," she murmurs. A pea-sized tear speeds down her cheek as she ruminates in her still stance.

I Want You to Know...

A plump, dark-olive-skinned femme with a raven-colored disheveled bun atop her head lies in a hospital bed. Her stout arms embrace a blanket-cocooned newborn girl. The baby's skin matches her mother's. Wisps of dark hair reveal from under her pink striped stretch cap adorned with a bow. She sleeps in contentment while her mother speaks:

I want you to know I love you. I just met you, yet you mean so much to me. Your tiny fingers, nose, and toes make me so happy.

My body carried you for nine months, but my soul has known you forever. You have been with me for so much, but you are barely a full day old. You were kicking me when I woke in the morning and lay on my bladder throughout the night. You made me gassy during the worst moments like when I stood in crowded elevators. As your tiny body grew, so did my ankles. He-he!

I dealt with snide comments from classmates while walking the halls from class to class.

"Is she pregnant? Eww."

"I heard it happened the night she lost her virginity."

"Look who's next to be on welfare. Ha-ha!"

You were not planned or expected, but you came from love. Is it crazy to say I didn't know love until I met you? I owe you my all and am forever in debt to you. You deserve to be spoiled with love, attention, a home, and family that can provide all of that for you.

Your life is worth more than I can afford. I have named you Luna because every night when I look up at the sky, I will lay in bed thinking of the precious baby girl I couldn't keep for myself. You will spend the rest of your life being loved by a couple that can give you the moon and beyond. Be great, my sweet star.

She kissed her Luna on the forehead and held her for one more minute.

Friday Night

After six Fridays in a row, the trip across town becomes second nature to John. He drives his shiny black coupe Deville with his old-school hip-hop blaring from the car's open windows. Eight blocks down Main Avenue followed by two rights and he is on Green Street at Blythe's brick townhouse. As he approaches her street, his throat takes a large gulp, his eyes blink rapidly, and he rehearses his drop off.

"Hey, there...here's your usual," he suavely plays out loud.

His eyes scan for an empty space between the parked cars on the street filled with sky-high townhomes.

He taunts himself, rethinking his previous deliveries that have failed to get him a date with Blythe.

"We gotta stop meeting up like this."

"Enjoy your dinner. See you next week!"

"So you like pizza. Aye?"

His eyebrows furrow on his forehead, and his face screws in disgust.

"I have no game whatsoever." He chuckles while taking calculated turns to swing between a minivan and a sedan.

The moment turns to a slow crawl.

He makes deliberate moves. John's buff right hand grabs the gear and pushes it forward shift by shift at a snail's speed. After the car is parked, his broad shoulders hoist his upper body toward the rearview mirror. He smiles while admiring his square chiseled jawline and straight white teeth. His head tilts downward, revealing his broad crooked nose. A constrained sigh reveals as he self-consciously acknowledges the snout on his face.

"The face only a mother could love." He grimaces to himself.

After taking a beat, John's left hand glides along the door panel, pressing the unlock button. The door swings open after he pulls the release handle and pushes it.

"Oh shit! I forgot the stupid seat belt," he jests.

After being restrained by the overlooked belt, John clicks the red button labeled "PRESS" to free himself from the vehicle. His legs swing to his left, hitting the pavement. His body glides out of the car, and he stands, angling his body toward the trunk. His feet take three large steps, and he's at the rear of his car. He presses the trunk release on the key fob and lifts the hood.

The aroma of a fresh pepperoni with double cheese pie and antipasto salad wafts under his nose. The smell reminds him of Blythe, minus her clementine-vanilla perfume, a fragrance that prickles his pecker.

He reaches into the trunk, grabbing the food to bring to his coveted delivery diva. A hint of pop radio filters to the street from a front window in Blythe's place. John eagerly walks toward her red door and presses the lit doorbell. The chime of the bell triggers his heart to throb. The music pauses. A white light illuminates through the diamond-shaped geometric window design. A blurry version of Blythe's straight dark hair and slim figure approaches.

"Hi," Blythe cheerfully greets after opening the door.

"Hey…uh…hi." John smiles back.

The moment pauses.

Blythe's eyes coyly stare upward at John's awestruck gaze. The pizza is fresh out the oven, but John's palms endure the heat while taking in his weekly moment to see Blythe. A minute later, the silence is broken by John's smartphone buzzing.

"It's probably just a text from my coworker," John assures.

"So I see you've got my usual," she says while motioning to take the pizza from John's hold.

"Uh, yeah, $23, please." John smiles.

His mouth opens to follow up with another comment, but Blythe cuts him off.

"As you can see, I really like pizza." She girlishly giggles.

"Ha, ha." John laughs.

"We gotta stop meeting up like this," Blythe teases.

"Heh." He grimaces, flustered by her witty banter.

Blythe pivots to her left and places the food on a nearby table. John takes the opportunity to reach into his pocket and read the message on his phone. She turns back and passes the cash to John. A bead of sweat appears and lingers at his right temple as his face turns crimson. His hand reaches forward to receive the cash from Blythe.

"Uh-hm. Enjoy your dinner. See you next week!" He nods and quickly speed walks away.

She watches him scurry to his car and closes the door.

The text message from his coworker Eric reads:

"Bro, stop with the lame lines, or you'll never get a date."

Laura's Loss

Ring. Ring. Ring. Click.

A smartphone rings, disconnecting when no one answers.

"I wonder what he's so busy doing that he has no time to answer the phone lately," a female voice mumbles.

Laura, a long-legged chocolate-toned slender woman sashays out of her luxury apartment inside a Manhattan midtown high-rise. She is fashioned in red open-toe pumps, medium-blue deconstructed jeans, a white T-shirt, and a fitted blazer. After five steps away from her door, she halts and pivots back in an agitated huff.

"Oh, come on, my key fob too?" Laura mumbles while her fingers comb through her purse, hunting for her car's remote.

As she reaches her door, her hand feels the metal L-shaped key ring attached to the key fob and nabs it out of her satchel.

"Ahhh," she sighs in relief. "One less item I'm losing this week."

Laura's white manicured hands move her tortoise-shell sunglasses from on top of her silky straight-haired head to her high cheek-boned face. She carries on with her catwalk down the brightly lit low-carpeted hall to the elevator.

Once she arrives, she stands next to her neighbor Mrs. Moore.

"It's going to be a lovely day outside, dear." Mrs. Moore curiously smiles and nods to Laura.

"Yeah. Uh, I guess so," Laura distractedly replies.

The silver doors open, and the women step into the lift that smoothly lowers them to the first level of the building. After a beat, the doors glide open and Laura swiftly steps forward to free herself from the box.

"Try to have a good day!" Mrs. Moore's concerned tone calls out to Laura.

She has left her neighbor in her dust. Her heels clack loudly against the paved walkway that leads her to the lower level parking deck.

Bing. Boop.

Laura's car lights up and responds to her clicker.

Laura's feet take a runway stride towards her polished navy sedan nestled in the sea of other luxury sedans, coupes, and sports utility vans. She swivels her slim waist left and right around the crowd of vehicles until she reaches her chariot and glides into the left driver's side.

"God, please get me through this day successfully," she pleads out loud while bowing her head down toward her tightly clasped hands. "Whatever you're trying to show me, please give me a sign."

Her gripped fingers release, and she presses the push start on her car.

"Tick, tick, err," the car whimpers out.

In disbelief, she tries again.

"Tick, tick, err, err."

Laura eyes her smartphone on the front passenger seat, grabs it, and scrolls through her contacts. Her fingers stop searching when she locates the number for the car emergency service.

"Hello," an auto service representative says.

"Hello. Hi," she says, cutting off the call rep's rehearsed lines. "I need someone to come now to check on my car."

"Okay, ma'am. What seems to be the problem?" he asks. "Do you need the car towed?"

"Yes. My car will not start. Can someone come here to fix it?" she requests.

"Ma'am, the best I can do is send a tow truck to bring your car to a local shop," the call center representative offers.

"How soon can they get here?" she anxiously asks. "I have an appointment in an hour that I cannot miss."

"Our system has tracked your phone call location," the representative pauses. The sound of keyboard taps echo in the background. "I can have someone at your location in…forty-five minutes."

"Ugh, no. That won't work," Laura says. Her eyes glaze over while staring into the distance. She pulls the phone away from her ear and presses the red illuminated button to end the call.

After a loud sigh, Laura pulls down the sun visor. She reviews her reflection and uses the tip of her pinky finger to wipe away her eye makeup that melted into the crease of her eyes from her near breakdown. After her beauty clean-up, she dials on her phone once more.

"Hello?" a deep suave male voice answers the call.

"Jason. Hey, honey. I'm having another bad day," she whines. "My favorite cat-eye sunglasses are missing, so I had to wear my round tortoise-shell shades. I thought I lost my car remote, but I had it. Then I got in the car, and it won't start…"

"Uh-h-h-h, sweetie, I have to call you later…," Jason cuts in.

The sound of a click followed by dead air hits a hard presence.

"Uh…" Laura loses her words.

After a beat, she gathers her handbag, opens the car door, slides out of the seat, and removes herself from the vehicle.

"Br-r-r-p-p-p." She puffs air through her lips, causing a drone sound. "And now it seems like I'm losing my boyfriend."

The car door closes, then she walks out of the parking deck toward the street. After reaching the sidewalk, her delicate fingers tap on the screen of her phone to request a lift to her destination via a ride-hailing mobile application.

Ten minutes later a green compact hatchback car arrives at Laura's curbside.

"Hi. Are you Laura?" the female driver asks through the front passenger window. She has a petite slim frame and straight, shoulder-length brown hair.

"Hello. Yes, I am," Laura states while opening the rear door and entering. Her right hand reaches to close the door.

Laura lies her head on the headrest and watches the bustling of New York City fly by as her chariot transports her to her destination.

"Is smooth jazz okay?" the driver asks while turning the radio on. Her eyes meet her passenger's through the rearview mirror.

"Yes. In fact, it is my favorite," Laura muses and continues to glance out the window.

"You seem pumped for an important meet-up," the driver continues. "Feel free to grab a bottled drink in the cooler near you. I'm Karmen by the way."

"Nice to meet you, Karmen," Laura replies after a sip of flavored seltzer water. "Yes, I am on my way to a major meeting."

"Sounds exciting. Is it for work?" Karmen asks.

"It is for my clothing designs," with pride, Laura reveals. "I want this more than anything."

"Doesn't it feel good to work hard for something and finally get it after all your effort?" Karmen suggests.

"Yes. I have always had a way about me where I set my eyes on something and I make it mine," Laura says smugly.

"So let me get this straight, even if it is not yours, you take it as long as you want it?" Karmen clarifies.

"Yes, I'm unstoppable," Laura delights. "I always get what I—" Laura's head sways and hits the window, and her eyes close.

Sometime later she awakens in a cold concrete-walled room. It reeks of stale urine and feces. Her mouth is gagged with a cotton cloth tied around her head, and her hands and feet are zip tied to a rickety wooden chair. There is an old rusted red garage door in front of her. Her head turns left to right up and down, observing the shelves surrounding her. She spots her favorite sunglasses, lucky bra, missing art portfolio, white-gold charm bracelet among other items she forgot about like her black satin headband, chunky yellow-gold anklet, and mobile tablet.

Laura's hands and feet frantically wiggle to attempt to escape, but none of them budge.

"*Help-p-p-p!*" Laura cries out, muffled under her muzzle.

Footsteps approach and stop at the garage door she sits behind. Laura wiggles and bounces in the chair to make noise and bring attention to herself.

"*Help me!*" she cries.

The door rises to overhead, revealing Karmen.

"Karmen? Help me!" she pleads.

"Oh no, bitch. I'm the reason you're here," Karmen assures with a smirk as she walks into the concrete box. She reaches up to lower the door and lets it fall behind her as she faces her hostage.

"Huh? Let me go! This is crazy!" Laura fearfully demands.

"No," Karmen says after an audible sigh. She nears hogtied Laura and unties her mouth.

"Why are you doing this?" Laura questions after licking her lips to bring moisture back to her mouth. "I haven't done anything to you."

Karmen ignores her counterpart and searches through her large duffle bag filled with tricks.

"You're crazy!" Laura screams. "I don't deserve this!"

"So I do?" Karmen lunges toward Laura and screams back.

"But I never did anything to you," Laura whimpers.

"Oh? Nothing?" Karmen debates. "Ms. I Make It Mine did nothing?"

"Listen, I see you have a lot of my belongings and I don't know why, but you can keep them and let me go, and I won't say anything," Laura offers.

"I don't want your stuff," Karmen nonchalantly says. "I just want to take your happiness."

"Well, I don't need those things. They are yours. You can have them all," Laura suggests.

"No. See, I just want you to feel how I feel," Karmen lectures. "You see, Jason—"

"Yes, my boyfriend Jason is going to be looking for me soon," Laura interrupts.

"Oh, honey. You mean, Jason, the man you knew was in a relationship but seduced anyway?" Karmen continues slyly.

"He and I are a good match," Laura debates.

"Wanna call him?" Karmen jokes on. "There's no signal here anyway."

"We are so good together. I am sorry. I didn't think of the other person I would be hurting," Laura pleads.

"Yes, you both match, just like your shoes and the garage door." Karmen laughs. "I don't want your things. Yes, I borrowed them, but now I'm giving them back to you." Karmen shrugs.

Laura's eyebrows furrow in puzzlement.

"As for your Jason, I already sent another woman to entertain him now. He most likely already forgot about you." Karmen smiles sinisterly.

"Why-y-y-y?" Laura sobs uncontrollably. "Why all this? I just want to get back to my life."

"And I just want my life back!" Karmen angrily scolds. "This is what I need to do to make things even. I'm giving you the stuff I stole back while your man leaves your life like how he left mine."

"So let me go!" Laura wails forcefully.

"No, honey. You and this garage door are a good match. I'll leave you both to be together," Karmen stoically replies.

She walks in reverse, watching Laura as she whimpers and sobs. She bends down to grab the door handle and lifts it to just above her head and steps out of the brick cube.

"By the way, this place is scheduled to be demolished tomorrow. Maybe your true match will find you," Karmen declares before closing the door in front of her. She walks away immediately, not looking back.

Determined to escape and survive a youthful demise, Laura bounces in the chair and wiggles until it falls on the side. The drop is intense, and the left wooden arm has broken off from the impact.

"Eh-h-h-ah!" Laura cries out in pain.

She realizes her arm is free and uses it to push her left ankle down the leg of the chair, leaving herself still wearing the zip tie.

"*Grrr*-urrr!" she grunts.

She does the same for the other ankle and limps over to the shelves, dragging the rest of the chair connected to her right arm. A skinny heel of black pumps on the shelf becomes the tool she uses to slide under the zip tie and gives her room to free her wrist. After a quick swoop of her satchel bag over her shoulder, she bends down to grab the door handle and lift it over her head. Laura hobbles from the stale cell down the hall and out the building's first floor door. Her feet are swollen. She stops once, leaving the condemned building, and takes her shoes off one by one.

"Argh!" she wails out in pain of relief. Her feet drag as she takes steps toward an opening in the metal chain link fence.

Her smartphone vibrates to signal that a text message has been received. Her slim hands weakly reaches into her bag and pulls out the phone. Its screen displays a message from Jason.

"We need to talk."

Knowing how the rest of that conversation will go, she stoically ignores it and continues walking.

CPSIA information can be obtained
at www.ICGtesting.com
Printed in the USA
LVHW011402300720
661946LV00002B/121